by Nora Ryan   Nora Ryan

To Kevin –
for the adventurous
Boys within!

Love Ryan

www.noraryanbooks.com

Designed and produced by Linda Mitsui.

ISBN-13: 978-1479299768
ISBN-10: 1479299766

ACKNOWLEDGMENTS

My thanks to Mary Billy and Margaret Ardan for their assistance in proof reading and editing. Margaret also shared chapters with her students and provided helpful feedback during the early development of the story. Special thanks to Sorcha and Daragh Collins O'Regan who read and approved the final copy. Their 8 and 10 year old perspectives were very encouraging.

To Linda Mitsui who has been a joy to collaborate with, my heartfelt thanks for breathing life into my dragons and their precarious predicaments!

Nora Ryan

To Brendan:

Who was the first to listen

and ask for more

as the adventure unfolded.

Contents

Dragon Quest

On the island of Frith there lived three young dragons, Ember, Spark and Soot. The sea around Frith is a spectacular purple. It is crystal clear except for a brief period each year when it turns green and freezes solid. Young dragons learn to fly during the freeze when the ice can support their weight and assist with clumsy landings. These are the days of Phoenix when all the young dragons display their dragoncrafts and if they are successful earn their quest pouches.

Ember, Spark and Soot attended Dragon Academy where Professor Blaze taught them in the ways of dragoncraft. Subjects essential to the mastery of dragoncraft are: Flight Theory, Flame Throwing and Dragon Code. Dragons are really too heavy to fly, except with the aid of strong wind currents. A good knowledge

Ember

Spark

Soot

of flight theory is the best way to succeed. Fortunately the weather in Frith is windy and one can see dragons flying most days except during Mogadon, when the wind dies down and even Professor Blaze is grounded.

Ember was a whiz at flight theory and he knew all the wing stretches, dips and flapping patterns. He practiced in the schoolyard every recess and was looking forward to the day when Professor Blaze would take the class to the practice cliff.

Spark was a natural at flame throwing. From a very early age he had learned to throw fireballs with great accuracy. This skill made him a favorite for the fizzbang team.

Soot was born with a loose fire-spurter. He couldn't control where any of his fireballs would go and they continually missed their target. His wings were underdeveloped for his age and though not impossible it was going to be difficult for him to fly. He was not looking forward to flight practice even though he knew his theory quite well.

He was very tall for his age and stood head and neck above the rest of his classmates. He was a most obliging dragon, and helped his classmates gather some of the choicest conkers from the highest branches of the conker trees.

These three dragons had been best friends since dragongarten and their friendship served them very well as we shall see.

Flight School

Our story begins on the morning of the first day of Phoenix. The dragons were all gathered on the slope leading to the edge of Gillies Cliff. Professor Blaze was in quite a flap giving last minute flight instructions to his students.

"Hurry along now, dragons," he urged. "The wind is blowing 20 knots from the north. It's a perfect morning for flight practice. The ice is thick enough but a bit rough. You must land heels first with your claws retracted or you will fall on your snout." Ember started to jump up and down practicing his heel landings. Spark was hopping around beside him spitting out mini fireballs. "Look, Ember," he puffed, "I'm going to blow some fire ahead of me as I come in to land to help smooth out the ice."

"My, my, what long nails you have Soot," remarked Professor Blaze as he strode past him. "Better keep those claws up. Right then, dragons," he said, turning his attention to the rest of the class, "Watch closely as I demonstrate."

Professor Blaze unfolded his wings, licked the tips with his long red tongue and started to do a running bounce towards the edge of the cliff. At the last second he straightened and stretched his neck out, sprang into the air and caught an updraft of breeze. The young dragons watched as he glided out over the bay, dipped his wings slightly and started a smooth descent to the ice surface, landing with ease.

He then hopped onto a large boulder, turned his snout into the wind, leapt into the air and flew back up to the cliff top.

When he got back to his students, he said, "Now, who is going to be first?" There was an awkward silence as the dragons examined their claws and licked their wings. It all seemed a bit scary. The wind coming in from the frozen sea had patches of swirling orange mist where it mixed with the warmer air at the top of the cliff. The ice was hissing and creaking and was a very long way down. Ember started to recite to himself the five points for beginner gliding and landing.

"That's right, Ember," chimed in Prof. Blaze. "Neck outstretched for take-off, wings balanced and level for flight, dipped for descent, heels down and snout up for landing. Off you go then," said Prof. Blaze.

Ember swallowed hard and started to bounce towards the cliff's edge.

"Faster," shouted Prof. Blaze and Ember picked up speed as he neared the edge.

"Wing tips up!" was the last thing he heard before jumping off the cliff. His eyes were closed and his heart thumped so loudly he could actually hear it. He felt the air rush against his wings as his body plunged downwards. He opened one eye and saw the ice rushing towards him and the mist swirling in the wind. He spread his wings as far apart as he could, clenched his fangs and uttered a dragon prayer. Then a warm air pocket lifted him up. He opened both eyes and saw that everything had slowed down. He was no longer hurtling towards the ice but slowly gliding towards the large red circle that Prof. Blaze had painted on the ice. As he got down closer to the surface he hit some cold air and

it bounced him around. "Keep your wings straight," roared Prof. Blaze. Ember stiffened his wings and straightened his flight. His heels were well stuck out in front of him as he came in to land and he slid along the ice with his tail grazing the surface as he came to a shuddering halt. *I made it!* thought Ember. *My tail is a bit sore – but I made it!*

His feet felt like jelly as he waddled to the nearest flat rock and sat down. Before long, he could see the rest of the dragons taking off one by one from the cliff. After a while as they all got a little braver, a few leapt into the air at the same time.

"One at a time" – shouted Prof. Blaze. "Dear, dear, this will not do at all," he muttered as he leapt out after them. A good thing too, because two young dragons collided on the way down and started to go into a tailspin. He swooped under them to stop their free-fall and coach instructions into their terrified ears until they slowed down, and resumed gliding normally.

Finally, Soot was the only one left. He stood trembling at the edge of the cliff. He'd seen Ember and Spark perform quite well and was about to jump just before the collision that could have ended in a catastrophe if it weren't

for Prof. Blaze's gallantry. *I don't think I can do it,* thought Soot. *I wish I hadn't eaten that extra plate of porridge this morning. I'm sure I'm too heavy.*

He looked down and could see all the others way below, waving their wings and encouraging him to jump. Prof. Blaze nodded his head and clapped his paws to encourage him. Tears of fear welled up inside of Soot. They squeezed their way through his tear ducts and started to flow uncontrollably down his thick leathery skin. *I can't do it. I just can't do it.* He poked his head under his wing and stood frozen to the spot. Some of the dragons on the beach started to snigger at him. Then, just as he was about to turn around and skulk home, Ember and Spark arrived at his side.

"We ran all the way back up the path from the beach," they puffed. "Come on, Soot, you can do it."

"Can't," said Soot, but he peeked out from under his wing and couldn't help just feeling a little less terrified now that his two friends were beside him.

"It's really fun!" said Ember. "Scary, but fun."

"See where that swirl of orange mist is?" said Spark.

"Uh –huh," said Soot.

"That's a warm air pocket. It will give you a big boost to get gliding." Soot waddled a little closer to the edge.

"You'll feel like you're dropping like a boulder at first," said Ember, remembering his scary launch, "– but if you keep your neck stretched out and your wings spread wide, that warm air pocket will slow you right down."

"Yeah," said Spark, "and then you'll be cruising, all they way to the big landing target on the ice." Soot looked down to the landing strip on the ice. He could see the rest of the dragons on the beach. They were collecting driftwood for a fire they had started and were getting set up for a gizzard roast. They had quite lost interest in him. Prof. Blaze, however, was still looking up at him, nodding his head and flapping his wings in an encouraging way. And Soot did love gizzards.

Suddenly, Ember sprang into the air, swooped downwards and caught the warm air pocket like a pro. Spark gave Soot ever so slight a nudge.

"You next," he said as he batted Soot's shoulder with his wing. The last thing that Soot wanted was to be left standing alone once again on top of the cliff. He leapt wildly into the air, stretching his neck out as far as it would go. Soot was a bit bottom heavy so it was very hard for him to stay horizontal. His body wanted to flip into a vertical tailspin. Spark was right behind him and every time Soot looked liked he was losing his glide and about to plummet, he would blow a great blast of fire and create just enough of a warm air pocket to give Soot a bit of a boost. Soot was wobbling quite a bit from side to side as his wings weren't quite large enough to keep his glide balanced. He held them stiffly, stretching them out as much as he possibly could. Ember, who was just a little ahead of him created a slipstream to help smooth out the path for him. In this way the three friends made their way down towards the ice. As they came close to the target, Prof. Blaze started to shout instructions.

"Prepare for landing. Dip your wings! You'll overshoot the target!" Ember and Spark dipped their wings, and started to make their landing. Soot's wings were stiffened into position and try as he might he couldn't budge them. He overshot the target and made his landing exactly where the ice and the beach met. His heels hit the ice and then an instant later dug into the sand, jolting him to a stop that toppled him forward onto his snout. He slid snout-first along the beach and he finally came to a stop a whisker's breadth from the campfire.

"A bit rough, but well done," laughed Prof. Blaze. Soot lay in the sand quite exhausted from the whole ordeal until some dragon shouted, "Gizzards and guts! Who wants some gizzards and guts?"

Soot could smell the deliciously pungent odor of barbecued gizzards and guts and he slowly pulled himself up to a sitting position and wiped the sand from his snout.

"Over here, please," he said and everyone laughed.

Skegg Island

For the next three days the dragons returned to the cliff to practice. The more they practiced, the stronger and more graceful their flight became. They noticed that their wings were becoming more flexible, and capable of making small adjustments to improve their balance and work the air currents. Even Soot noticed the change. In fact, he suspected that his wings might have even grown a little as he could now touch his claws with the tips of his wings—or was it because he was becoming more flexible? He had discovered that he could use his long neck to counter his tendency to flip and though he was not as fast as the other dragons he was making a good deal of progress. He was quite pleased with himself.

To pass flight school each dragon had to make an accurate landing on the target and they had to fly from Gillies Cliff to Skegg Island and back. All the dragons had passed their first test by the end of day two. Skegg Island wasn't very far. It was just four dragon breaths from the edge of Gillies Cliff. The

problem was it was surrounded in thick green fog. The dragons had to time their landing to correspond with four dragon breaths exactly – no more and no less. If the dragons flew too far, too fast they would crash into the island. If they miscalculated and engaged their landing position too soon they would fall into the sea. The sea around Skegg Island never froze and as sea take-offs were for expert flyers only that was not an option for these dragons.

Once again, Prof. Blaze gave a demonstration.

"Now watch carefully," he warned. "Count my breaths and the number of wing flaps it takes for me to fly to the end of my breath. All dragon breaths are the same length – but the number of flaps each dragon has to make to get to the end of the breath varies. Count mine." Prof. Blaze took three running bounces towards the cliff edge before taking off. Just before take-off he blew a long lick of flame to mark his breath. The dragons started to count...one flap...two flaps...three flaps... just then Prof. Blaze emitted another burst of flame.

"Three, three!" they shouted. And again... one flap...two flaps...three flaps. Prof. Blaze had a three flaps per breath glide.

"Three, three!" they shouted again. On the second flap of his fourth breath Prof. Blaze disappeared into the fog. There was an eerie silence as all the dragons held their breath and then a great big dragon whoosh of stale gizzard breath as Prof. Blaze emerged back through the fog flapping gracefully back to Gillies Cliff.

The order of go was drawn. Spark was first up. He did a few practice circles to check how many flaps per breath he made. He figured four.

"It's four, Prof. Blaze, isn't it?" he asked.

"Yes, Spark, it's four for you, so dip your wings and stick your heels out on the third flap of your fourth breath." Spark set off blowing his flame breath ahead of him.

One… two… three… four… Breath! One… two… three… four Breath! He was half way across. One…two…three…four… Breath! He could feel the warmer air as he approached Skegg Island. He was lifted up by an unexpected air pocket and propelled into the fog. It felt sticky and hot. One …two… three…*dip wings, dip wings!* He reminded himself, *heels out* – squish! Spark came to an abrupt halt with his claws stuck in a sticky green mound of something both slimy and smelly. He could hear the weirdest, raspiest, high-pitched laugh off to one side. As he tried to pull his claws out of the glue-like substance, he noticed that there were bubbles forming on the ground where the weird noise was coming from. Up from the bubbles popped a shiny wet green-headed thing that was blowing green slimy bubbles. Some of the bubbles floated towards Spark and as they hit him they burst and transformed into more of the gooey green

mess. Spark pulled and tugged until he finally got his claws free. He bounced to the edge of the island and lunged into his take-off as quickly as he could. The other dragons cheered as they saw him emerge through the fog. His flight was slower this time as the sticky green goo weighed him down. Spark struggled to keep going.

He was losing height with every breath. On his fourth breath it looked like he was going to fall short of the edge of Gillies Cliff.

"Quick, hold my tail, Ember," yelled Soot. Ember grabbed his tail.

"Yes, yes, form a chain," urged Prof. Blaze. With six dragons hanging off his tail, Soot leaned out over the cliff and stretched his long neck out and down so that Spark could grab it before he hit the cliff. Spark folded his wings around Soot and held on for dear life as Soot swung him safely up to the cliff's edge.

"Thanks, Soot, I thought I was a goner," said Spark as he unfolded his wings and slid to the ground.

"What's that awful smell," the dragons asked as soon as they had caught their breaths.

"Glomgoyl goo," said Prof. Blaze. "O dear, this is very bad news indeed," he said. "We thought they were all gone."

"Glomgoyl? What's a glomgoyl?" they asked.

"Glomgoyls are a species of dragon without any couth whatsoever," answered Prof. Blaze. "Several eons ago they lost their ability to fly and throw flames. Originally they inhabited the faraway continent of Smorgasland. It was a beautiful place and had everything a dragon could possibly want. Brisk winds, tall caves, lots of gizzards and even a plentiful supply of shoggies…"

"Oooooh, shoggies!" the young dragons exclaimed. "We're not allowed to eat those, are we, Prof. Blaze?"

"Certainly not! They are essential for removing the fog. This is precisely why there is so much fog around Skegg Island. No shoggies."

"Why did they lose their ability to fly?" asked Spark in between the warm puffs of air he was blowing on the goo to dry it before shaking it off.

"Shoggies live on the shoreline, sitting on the rocks all day absorbing the heat of the sun. At night they slowly release the heat keeping the temperature fairly constant so there is no fog build up. The glomgoyls kept excavating their caves to make them bigger and bigger so that there was eventually no room for the shoggies. They also ate them in large numbers. They are pretty easy to catch, as you know. Some of the shoggies migrated to other lands but most of them died off. For a while the glomgoyls kept the fog banks away by using there own breaths to warm the atmosphere but eventually they ran out of flame and the fog got thicker and thicker until they could no longer fly in it. They still had their big caves and their herds of gizzards but their wings got smaller and smaller until they disappeared altogether." Soot looked at his wings and wondered if he might have any glomgoyls in his ancestry. He certainly hoped not. "I wonder how they got to Skegg Island?" said Prof. Blaze, thinking out loud. "The rest of you will need to be very careful where you land. Glomgoyl goo plays havoc with your glide, throws it all out of whack. Stay over by the west side of the island where I landed," he advised.

The rest of the dragons were not nearly as enthusiastic about the flight to Skegg Island but they were a plucky lot and all wanted to graduate from flight school. One by one they flew to Skegg Island keeping as far away from where Spark had entered the fog bank as they could. A few came back with green splotches of glomgoyl goo and Prof. Blaze hovered around the cliff edge ready to give a boost to any dragon who was having difficulty flying. Ember covered the distance in record time and gave Soot some very helpful advice.

When Soot headed off he discovered that his breath was five flaps. The first three breaths went fine with his fireballs coming out both strong and straight. When he got close to the fog bank he felt a rumbling in the back of his throat. When he tried to blow his last burst of flame his fire-spurter started to quiver. His breath came out like a firecracker throwing sparks in every direction. At first this scared him but he discovered that the sparks cleared the fog and he was able to find a nice landing spot. He didn't see any glomgoyls but he saw several gooey green mounds and could feel their presence. A cloud of glomgoyl bubbles floated towards him but when they landed on him they didn't burst and become sticky as had happened with the other dragons. They bounced right off him. The scales on the back of his neck started to tingle with fear. Something very weird was happening. He turned around and leapt back into the fog, spurting out sparks in every direction until he cleared the fog bank. Then he flew back to the other dragons as fast as he could.

"Well done, dragons. You have all passed your flight test," announced Prof. Blaze.

"Hooray! Hooray!" shouted the young dragons, jumping up and down and flapping their wings in excitement.

"Tomorrow we will practice our flame throwing. Now, I must hurry back and inform the dragon council about the glomgoyls on Skegg Island."

Fizzbang

Spark, Ember and Soot were very pleased as they headed home, especially Soot who was feeling a lot more like a regular dragon, now that he had passed his flight test. *Perhaps with practice,* he thought, *I can improve my flame throwing as well.* The three friends decided to play fizzbang on the way home. Three of the other dragons, Wrinkles, Jade and Scorcher joined in to form an opposing team. Each team got ten minutes to gather as many conkers as they could and then they set up their defenses on either side of Cliffside Road. The object of the game was to hurl the conkers at each other and the opposing team would try to burn them in mid-air before they landed on the other side.

As the conkers started to fly the dragons blew flames as far and as quickly as they could to catch the incoming conkers. Spark was bouncing all over the place shooting out fireballs with great accuracy. Ember had a careful aim and hit all the conkers he blew flame at but because he was slow missed a few. Soot was desperately spurting out as much flame as he could but it didn't go very far and

most of the incoming conkers on his end hit the ground out of range of his fireballs. To make matters worse some of his flame was so off-target that he brought down a few of his own team's conkers. *That* was very embarrassing. At the end of the game Spark had a perfect score with no conkers by his feet, Ember had three and Soot had nine for a total of twelve. The other dragons had nine in total and had a good laugh at the heap lying close to Soot.

"Sure you're not a glomgoyl?" snickered Scorcher as he passed by Soot with his tail swishing in a bragging sort of way.

"Yeah, smells a bit like one too," said Wrinkles sniffing the air as he passed.

Jade didn't say anything just followed the other two in silence. Spark, Ember and Soot stood in line with their wings raised in a dragon salute to show respect to the opposing team as they passed by.

"Well," hissed Ember under his breath, "that's not very couth, they never gave the dragon salute at the end of the game, maybe they're the ones with glomgoyl relatives."

"It's only a game," laughed Spark. "Who cares!"

Soot cared. He wanted to pass flame throwing and to earn his dragon pouch. Later that evening he asked his mother a question - a question that had been on his mind a lot lately.

Soot Learns about his Father

"Mother, what was my father like?"

"Your father was a very brave dragon. He had great loyalty to his dragon clan and as you know was lost at sea in a fog storm during a daring expedition in search of new lands."

"Yes, Mother, but what did he look like?"

"Well, umm, he was big of course, being a Bremmen. His wing span was a bit short but his wings were so powerful that he became a top flyer even with this, umm, slight defect."

"What colour was he, Mother?"

"Well, he was a very dark shade of green, quite unusual really, for a Bremmen. What's gotten into you, Soot? Why all the questions? The most important thing you need to know about your father is that he was a loyal and faithful dragon."

"Glomgoyls are green, aren't they, Mother?"

"Glomgoyls? Glomgoyls! Where did you hear about glomgoyls?" Soot told his mother the whole story about the expedition to Skegg Island, how Spark had gotten covered in glomgoyl goo and how they had all passed their flight test – barely.

"You passed flight school. That's wonderful, Soot," she burst in, unable to contain herself. "I'm so proud of you."

"Why did Father not come back?" asked Soot, changing the subject back to his father. "Did he not want to come back to us?"

"Of course he did, Soot. Whatever made you think that?"

"It's not fair," he sobbed. "I can't throw a fireball as far as the ditch. All the other dragons practice with their fathers every evening. I'm a laughing stock. It's not fair!"

"When you were very young, Soot, your father took you to Harroby Marsh to watch him practice his flame throwing."

"But it's so long ago, I don't remember."

"All that he taught you is still with you. It is your challenge to tap into it. Come with me, Soot," she said and quietly flew up to the loft.

A week ago Soot would not have been able to follow but now his wings were strong and he made it to the loft with one bounce and two flaps. Tucked away under an old beam was a wooden chest, which his mother pulled out to the middle of the floor and opened. As soon as she opened it, Soot's scales started to tingle. The smell coming from the chest was definitely a glomgoyl smell. He felt his throat tighten and his heart pound. His mother took out a pouch made of gizzard leather.

"This was your father's quest pouch," she said touching it gently. "It was found floating in the Sea of Goluth many hundreds of dragon breaths from here."

"But it smells like …. like…. glomgoyl," he whispered.

"During the fog storm all the dragons went off-course. Some of them, including your father landed on a remote island. They decided to wait out the storm there before continuing on. At first they thought it was uninhabited. But soon they discovered that glomgoyls were on the island. A terrible battle ensued. The glomgoyls wanted to steal the quest pouches. You see, Soot, the strength of a dragon lies hidden in his quest pouch. The glomgoyls hoped that by stealing the quest pouches they would regain their ability to fly and breathe fire."

"What happened?" asked Soot.

"Although there were many glomgoyls, the dragon warriors were faster, fiercer and could fly and throw flame. The glomgoyls asked for a truce. Your father was sent to negotiate. The glomgoyls offered food to the dragons during the peace talks. But it was a trick. The food was drugged and they were all captured. One of the dragons managed to escape and made it back to Frith. A large search party went out to find the island but it had mysteriously vanished. Your father's pouch was found floating in the location where they expected to find the island. The pouch was empty."

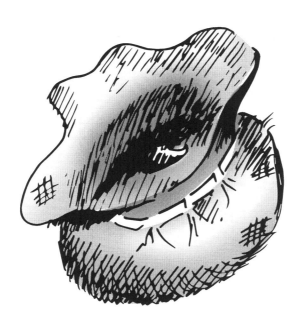

Soot examined the pouch carefully. The leather was thick and of a very fine quality but badly scratched with deep nicks in some areas. As he turned it over he noticed something stuck deeply into one of the nicks.

"There's something stuck in the pouch," he said showing it to his mother.

Soot used one of his claws to pry the object out and to his amazement as it came free it settled neatly over his clawnail.

"It's a clawnail," he exclaimed.

"Let me see," said his mother. She bent down and sniffed it. A huge teardrop fell from her snout. "It's your father's. He must have lost it while trying to hang on to his pouch."

Soot started to sniff at the clawnail. He could still smell glomgoyl but behind that smell was another smell, a soft earthy smell that reminded him of walks down by Harroby Marsh. He stretched out his claw so that his mother could remove his father's clawnail from it but it had bonded to Soot's clawnail and the two clawnails now looked like one.

"He's still alive! Your father is still alive," she exclaimed. "Only the nail of a living dragon can bond to another and it will only bond to kin. So now we know of a certainty that it is your father's."

"What are we going to do, now?" asked Soot.

"For now, you must say nothing of this to anyone. The dragon council has closed the case and will consider it of no consequence unless we have evidence of the existence and whereabouts of the island."

"But we must DO something! …I…*I* must do something."

"Soot, your job is to earn your quest pouch and to complete your quest. This is where your real strength lies. Only when you have the strength will you be able to help your father."

Harroby Marsh

The dragons spent the next four days practicing their flame throwing down at Harroby Marsh. By the fifth day, the day of testing, the air was full of smoke and the smell of sizzling gizzard juice. Gizzard juice enhances the colour of flame and many dragons mistakenly believe that it also helps them blow longer flames.

There were three tests to pass: length, accuracy and multiple balls. Prof. Blaze marked out the finishing line by scorching the grass with his breath. He sprinkled some gizzard juice along the scorch-line. The juice caused flame to burn a bright blue as it passed over the gizzard vapour. Each dragon had one practice throw (which didn't count) and then three attempts to cross the line, two of which had to be successful. Some of the dragons, such as Spark and Scorcher were very skilled at this event and their flames flew so high over the finish mark that they failed to light up the gizzard juice. Of course, anyone with half a dragon's eye could see that they had easily cleared the mark.

"Mine went the furthest," bragged Scorcher.

"See the S-shaped tail coming from its scorch mark? That's the Scarlew brand. We're the record holders for flame throwing."

Spark wasn't convinced and he looked at Prof. Blaze.

"I believe mine went further," said Spark.

"These are trials not a competition. You either pass or fail," he answered. "You have both passed. Next!"

Soot shuffled up to the start line. He couldn't believe his bad luck. Imagine having to throw right after Scorcher and Spark. He started to clear his fire-spurter.

"Harr, harr, ahouaghhrrhh!" he snorted.

Scorcher started to snicker.

"Relax and take a deep breath. You'll be fine," whispered Spark. But Soot was already turning a deep shade of purple from his efforts. He was anything but relaxed. He took a quick gulp of air and blew out the most pathetic arch of flame of the entire four days. It landed in a fizzle less than half way across and barely singed the grass where it landed. Scorcher squealed with laughter but Prof. Blaze silenced him with a wave of his wing.

"Dragon code, dragon code," he warned. Soot took another breath and blew as hard as he could. The flame shot out of his mouth with good speed but without enough lift and arched to the ground just short of the mark. Soot started to panic. He only had two shots left and both had to be successful to pass. He could feel his whole neck and throat wobbling uncontrollably. He put his claw around his neck to try to stop the wobbling. As soon as his father's clawnail touched his scales he started to feel a warm pulse coming from it. The pulse rippled through his skin and went deep down into his throat as far as his spurter. His spurter relaxed. His throat relaxed. He took a long deep breath and lifted his snout skywards, releasing a perfectly arched flame that blazed a deep blue as it crossed the finish line. The rest of the dragons sighed in amazement.

"That was a fluke! – Bet you can't repeat

it," whispered Scorcher, not wanting to be heard by Prof. Blaze. Soot was oblivious to both the impressed sighs of his friends and the teasing of Scorcher. In some mysterious way, he had connected with his father. *Thank you, Father,* he thought. *I will not let you down.* He closed his eyes, took another deep breath and blew an arch of flame of great beauty and proportion, which landed deep into the marsh at the far side of the finish line. There was a moment of silence and then all the dragons started to slap their wings in approval.

"Bravo! Pass!" exclaimed Prof. Blaze, unable to conceal his own excitement at this incredible turn of events.

Next came the accuracy tests. All the dragons formed a circle. A barrel of uncooked gizzard sausages was placed in the centre. The bottom of the barrel was spring-loaded and it released the gizzards one at a time quite irregularly and in all different directions. The

dragons had to take turns barbecuing the gizzard sausages as they twirled around in the air. This test took quite a bit of concentration but by now the dragons were hungry and very much looking forward to taking a lunch break. It's remarkable how the promise of a well-cooked gizzard sausage can focus the mind of young dragon warriors. Soon there was a big steaming pile of gizzard sausages in the centre of the circle and the sour smell of uncooked gizzard juice was changed into the very pleasant (for dragons anyway) aroma of sizzling gizzard sausages.

"My, my," chortled Prof. Blaze. "You have done well. Time for lunch!" Prof. Blaze distributed the gizzard sausages and all the dragons feasted heartily, then rolled onto their backs, curled their tails over their bellies, folded their wings on top and fell asleep.

While they were sleeping a very peculiar thing happened, very peculiar indeed. A thin finger of fog spiraled in from the sea. Along with it came a cloud of purple rain, most unusual for the time of year. As the rain fell on the marsh it came in contact with the very warm air created from all the flame throwing, causing the fog to become even thicker. By the time the dragons awoke they could barely see their clawnails.

Prof. Blaze could sense a wave of nervous fear wafting over the young dragons. He used his red-eye beam to check on the position of each dragon and to determine the length of the fog bank. He started to organize the dragons in groups of three. Soot, Ember and Spark were very relieved to find themselves in the same group.

"Don't worry, dragons," he declared. We will use our fireballs to dissipate the fog. This will be a cooperative trial. If you work together you will have enough fireballs to clear a track in the fog as far as Gillies Road. By then the visibility will be clear again. But we need to move fast. The groups of three were scattered all over the marsh. Prof. Blaze flew from group to group giving them flying directions and setting them on their way.

Ember was first to lead for his group. He sprang into the air, closely followed by Spark and Soot. Ember blew a burst of fireballs that made a hole in the fog two dragon breaths in length. The dragons flew into the hole and followed along its course. It was like flying through a tunnel. The sides of the tunnel were a sheet of dense fog. Just before they hit the wall of fog at the end of the tunnel, Spark moved forward and blew a great big gush of fireballs that lit up the sky just long enough to see the mayhem all around them. There were dragons flying in all directions, some of them quite disoriented and off-course. Then the tunnel formed again and the three dragons entered it and flew forward. The fog was soupy, thick and green. It was a very scary situation. Spark blew one more burst of fireballs and the three dragons flew deeper into the fog tunnel. Then Soot came up to take his turn. He was quite nervous. He had no idea how things might turn out. His flame throwing was so erratic. *Give me a sign, Father. How should I do this?* he whispered, scratching his head with nervous tension. Once again his father's clawnail made contact with his skin and Soot could feel his presence. Soot's vision became more focused and he could just make out a slight bend in the tunnel ahead. Soot curved his fireballs in the direction of the curve and started to veer towards the curve.

"What are you doing, Soot?" shouted Ember who was right behind him. Prof. Blaze told us to stick to a course directly north and now you are veering us to the east."

"I'm pretty sure it's the right thing to do – just trust me," he said. The dragons didn't have much choice because it was the only way to go where they could see anything. Soot blew one more burst of fireballs. As they sparked and lit up the surrounding area, Soot could see below him three dragons huddled in a pile on the wet marsh. Then the tunnel formed again but this time it was wider and the wall of fog seemed less dense. By the time Ember came up to take his turn at blowing fireballs they could see a clearing and the rocky outline of Gillies Road.

"You two, go on," said Soot. "I'm going back." Before they could protest, he had turned around and was flying back into the dense fog. He could feel all his senses growing powerful. His wings were beating harder, his nose could smell where the other dragons were and his eyes were emitting a red glow that helped him see through the fog. Red-eye vision was only possessed by full-blooded Bremmens, such as Prof. Blaze and his father and even then only after years of perfecting the technique. As he got closer to the three dragons stuck in the marsh, he could see that one of them had sunk deep into the mud and the other two were trying hard to pull him out. Every time they dug their claws in to get a good grip they also started to sink into the mud. Soot decided it was too dangerous for him to land.

"Grab my tail," he shouted as he hovered low over them lowering his long tail towards the ground. The dragon closest tried grabbing it with his front claws but they wouldn't quite reach. He tried again, reaching with his claws like a cat trying to catch a ball of wool – but without success. In the meantime the dragon stuck in the mud was yelling at them to – "pull harder, pull harder!" His wings were flapping against the mud as he tried in vain to work free of the sticky substance. Soot flew as low as he dared without losing the airfoil that kept him in the air. The dragon in the mud spread his wings over the other two dragons and started to haul himself up as Soot came closer. He opened his mouth and snapped at Soot's tail catching it in a very tight and painful grip

with his teeth. Soot snapped his tail back as a dagger of pain shot up his tail. There was a squelching sound as the stuck dragon (who turned out to be none other than Scorcher) came loose from the mud and was pulled up into the air by Soot. The other two dragons were now stuck in the mud and couldn't move.

"Flap your wings, Scorcher," shouted Soot, "or we'll both fall back into the swamp." Scorcher started to flap his wings and the drag on Soot lightened a bit. "Let go of my tail, Scorcher. I have to go back and help the other two." But Scorcher wouldn't let go. Soot started to swing his tail up and down and from side to side trying to rid himself of Scorcher. It wasn't until they reached the area where the fog was getting lighter that Scorcher finally let go and started to fly in a panic towards Gillies Road. Soot was really tired now and desperately wanted to land on Gillies Road and take a rest. But he knew the other two dragons were sinking into the marsh and he had to go back to save them. Once again he turned back into the dense fog and with the help of his red-eye vision found his way back to the other two dragons. They were stiff with cold by the time he got to them. The two loyal friends had wrapped their wings around each other to try to stay warm. This gesture had probably saved their lives because their wings now formed an umbrella shape that helped them from sinking too far into the mud. Soot could see that they could barely move let alone fly. He managed to curl his tail around the tail of the taller of the two and slowly – ever so slowly – lifted them out of the mud. They were now dangling from his tail, still clutching on to each other. *I can't carry them all the way back,* he thought. *I've got to find a way to warm them up quickly.* He turned and coughed out a very

small fireball in their direction - big enough to heat them but too small to burn them.

He could feel them wriggle and start to make little grunting noises. He wasn't sure if this was a good or a bad sign but he had no choice. He was now flying so low that one of the dragons was bumping off the ground every time Soot took the slightest break in flapping. He tried another small fireball.

"Ouch!" squealed the taller of the two and he suddenly shook himself free and started to flap his wings. The other little guy was still attached but starting to look around trying to figure out where he was and what was happening.

"It's okay," assured Soot, "you're almost at Gillies Road. Just flap as hard as you can." He tried to flap. One wing worked but the other was dragging loosely by his side. Poor little reptile had a broken wing and his efforts were very little use. Soot kept going. He was now so tired that his fireballs fizzled out quickly and the fog started to engulf them. His eyes were swollen from straining and his red-eye vision had very little penetration. But he could hear distant voices and kept flying towards them. Suddenly he hit something very hard and everything went black.

The next thing he remembered was waking up in his bed of moss with his mother and Prof. Blaze by his side.

"Soot!" cried his mother. "We were so worried about you. Are you okay?"

"Whaa—what happened?" asked Soot.

"Don't you remember?" asked Prof. Blaze.

"No," replied Soot. "But my head hurts and my tail is sore."

"You literally, fell out of the sky," said Prof.

Blaze. "You came crashing down on Gillies Road and knocked yourself out. You're lucky that Scorcher spotted you. He dragged you to the gathering area with the help of Wrinkles and Jade."

"He did?"

"Yes, he did. He also helped the Breggan brothers who were half frozen and delirious. Lucky for them that Scorcher was on their team. He pulled them out of the mud. They would probably have died without his help."

"What about Ember and Spark," asked Soot.

"Are they okay?"

"They're fine," said Prof. Blaze. "They were worried sick about you. Had the dragons running along the edge of the fog bank looking for you. What possessed you to fly back into the fog?"

"I don't know. I don't remember."

"Hmm," said Prof. Blaze. "This has been a very peculiar turn of events. Fog drifting in from the sea during the Days of Phoenix. Glomgoyls on Skegg Island. Very peculiar, and very troublesome. So much to tell the council, so much to tell the council," he muttered as he turned to leave.

Festival of Phoenix

The Frith Outdoor Arena was crowded with dragons of all ages and rank. A meteor that crashed on Frith many eons ago had scooped out a nice rounded bowl-shaped crater. The crater made a perfect natural arena for the games held during the Festival of Phoenix. The bottom of the crater served as the playing field and the sides were used as the viewing area for spectators.

The guard dragons were lined up at either side of the arena entrance, welcoming dragons as they arrived and showing them to their viewing areas. The parent dragons were squatting close to the field where they could see close at hand their young dragons playing fizzbang or flying through an obstacle course set up to show off their flight skills. This year's young graduates were a bit subdued compared to former years. Their frightening experience at Harrowby Marsh had left them bruised and a little less confident. Many had lost their way or had crash-landed as they tried to navigate through the fog. Not so, for a couple of brothers from the Scarlew clan who had been credited with the rescue of Soot, among others. They were strutting around confidently waiting for the game of fizzbang to start. Spark and Ember were in the centre of the arena but Soot was on the sidelines with his mother, a bandage of seaweed tied securely around his eyes to protect them from the flash of fireballs that would occur during the game. Ever since his accident at Harroby

Marsh, his eyes had been very sore and weepy. Prof. Blaze had advised that they stay covered for a full five Frith rotations. This meant that he couldn't participate in the games. As he had completed the flight and fire trails, he was eligible to graduate. But he was gloomy and puzzled. After all his hard work, he was stuck on the sidelines with his mother. He loved his mother, but when it came to dragon games and graduation, he missed having his father there. He was puzzled that he couldn't remember what happened at Harroby Marsh. What was even stranger was that though his eyes were weepy and sore he could still see through the seaweed bandage. He kept this to himself. He was quite enough of a freak as it was, what with his small wingspan and his unreliable fire-spurter. The dragon guards blew three loud blasts on their conch horns and the crowd fell silent.

Spoargum, the dragon king spoke from his perch on top of the carved pole in the middle of the arena. He had once been a very large, magnificent dragon with glorious bronze skin that quite set him apart. He had a wingspan twice the length of his tail and had been the strongest and fastest flyer in all of Frith for

many eons. He still looked imposing, but his wings now drooped a bit and the shiny bronze colour had turned a mottled brown and purple.

"Welcome to the Festival of Phoenix, dragons," he announced. "We are here to celebrate the graduation of our newest batch of dragon cadets. We know that blah, blah, blah....... It was the same speech that he had given every year for the past twenty thousand festivals. No one was listening, so it is impossible to record exactly what he said. A good time for most of the crowd to lie on their backs, fold their wings and take a little dragon nap while Spoargum retold the heroic deeds of previous eons of dragon warriors. Campaigns that no one remembered. Blah, blah, blah ... Glomgoyls on Skegg Island ... What? Glomgoyls? Glomgoyls! All the older dragons woke with a start and jumped to their hind legs. There was a lot of muttering about danger and wickedness and then suddenly – three loud blasts from the conch horns. Complete silence fell upon the crowd.

Spoargum swayed on the perch and bellowed out a warning. "We are no longer alone. The loathsome glomgoyls have reached close to our shores. A small band of them, probably scouts, is entrenched on Skegg Island."

"What are we going to do?" shouted some dragon from the crowd.

"Send a dragon squadron to Skegg Island," suggested another. "We all know those wingless creatures can neither fly nor swim."

"A- hmm a- hmm," Spoargum cleared his throat. "Dragons no longer go to war. Couth is our code – courtesy, cooperation and courage."

"We'll cooperate alright," shouted Scorcher's father – cooperate to push the glomgoyls into the sea." Several dragons laughed at this but overall there was a cold feeling of disquiet.

"There will be a special meeting of the council elders tonight," announced Spoargum. "There is no immediate danger. No immediate danger, whatsoever. Glomgoyls can't fly and the sea is unfrozen around Skegg Island. In another two days all of the ice between here and Skegg Island will have melted. In the meantime, we have posted guards at the edge of Harroby Marsh, the only possible place where the glomgoyls could come ashore if by some chance they found their way onto the ice-flow. I repeat. There is no immediate danger. Let the games begin!"

At that, the atmosphere lightened a little and the dragon guards blew the conch one more time to start the game of fizzbang. Immediately, the young dragons started to hurl their supply of conkers at each other while at the same time blowing flames to neutralize the incoming conkers. Prof. Blaze had divided the graduates into two well-matched teams for the exhibition game. Scorcher was the captain of one side and Spark was the captain of the other side. This made for an exciting match as the dragons huffed, puffed, jumped from side to side, dodged, twisted and generally went berzerk trying to outdo each other. As soon as a dragon had used up his pile of conkers he would continue throwing fireballs to assist his teammates, until the incoming conkers were finished. Scorcher as we know was particularly good at this game and had taken down most of his opponent's conkers as well as hurling his supply of conkers well into the opposing team's end zone. As soon as he had finished throwing his supply of conkers, he started to pirouette and flap his wings in a self-congratulatory manner, quite forgetting his teammates who were still trying to take down incoming conkers.

"Incoming conkers! Incoming conkers!" Jade shouted, who was on the same team and desperately trying to torch the stray conkers that his teammates had missed. Meantime, Prof. Blaze was running up and down the sidelines coaching both sides.

"Heads up! Heads up, Scorcher," he warned just as a stray conker came whirring in his direction and hit Scorcher smack between the eyes, knocking him out. That's the thing about dragons, tough as old boots all over their leathery surface except for that spot between their eyes. The skin is soft and flexible between the eyes to allow for the very rapid pulsing that occurs while red-eye vision is being used.

Ever noticed how close together a dragon's eyes are? That's to protect the soft spot. Prof. Blaze blew his conch.

"We'll have to stop the game," he announced as two dragon guards dragged Scorcher off the field. "It's against the code to play with unequal numbers."

"But it's also part of the code to play fizzbang in the Frith arena to determine who gets their dragon pouches first," complained Spark. Now that Scorcher was out of the picture his team had a chance to win. Soot yanked on his mother's wing.

"Bring me over to Prof. Blaze, please," he said. His mother escorted him onto the field.

"May I play as a substitute for Scorcher, Prof. Blaze," he asked.

"But you can't see with that bandage on. It's too dangerous," he replied. "One dragon out for the count is quite enough."

"I just need to throw flames to defend against incoming conkers," he argued, "and my bandage will protect me if I do take a hit. Though I'm pretty sure I won't," he added. Prof. Blaze looked up at the sun. It was just two dragon breaths above the rim of the arena.

"Very well," he agreed. "As there's very little time left, you can take his place." Prof. Blaze led Soot to Scorcher's position and then

blew his conch to restart the game. Soot jumped up and down, waggled from side to side as he blew out his fireballs in every which way he could. His fire-spurter was back to its old wobble again and some of his fireballs were very weak indeed, but every third or fourth one would burst out like a firecracker and take down several conkers. When the final conch blew there was a mess of burnt and un-burnt conkers to be counted on both sides. It was a close call but thanks to Soot's last minute efforts, Scorcher's side was still ahead.

"Hooray! Hooray!" the crowd shouted. "Scorcher's side wins. Line honours to Soot."

The other team, lead by Spark, lined up to give the dragon salute as Scorcher's team, now led by Soot filed up to the foot of Spoargum's pole.

"What did you do that for?" hissed Spark as Soot passed him. "Whose side are you on?"

"It's only a game, remember, Spark," replied Soot.

As dragon cadets slowly filed past Spoargum's pole, Prof. Blaze presented each one with his or her own personal pouch and quest scroll. Each pouch contained three small pebbles, individually wrapped in lizard tongue leather. The scroll contained instructions on the object of their quest. Each quest was unique to the dragon receiving it. After the presentations the cadets held their pouches high as they marched around the arena to thunderous applause from the spectators. Then Spoargum spoke:

"All dragon cadets must complete their quest and return here by the time the purple moon rises over Skegg Island. Read carefully the guidance you have received. It is the secret to your success."

The Quest

Later that evening, when Soot was alone in his lair, he unrolled his scroll. It read as follows.

Quest for cadet 13069 son of Stingfire and Fanfan

Before the purple moon has risen nine dragon breaths over Skegg Island bring to Spoargum:

Four lengths of gossamer from the giant red spider

Two crystal eggs from a sitting shoggie

The unspoiled skin of a tiger lizard

Soot shivered at the thought of going on the quest. He knew he would have to venture deep into Harroby Marsh to have any chance of success. Harroby Marsh was where the giant spiders lived – though he personally had never seen one. He had seen lots of brown lizards in the marsh. They were plentiful enough. But he had never seen a tiger lizard. They were known to be very shy creatures. Orange with brown stripes, and a glossy skin that they shed once in a lifetime when they changed from land creatures to sea creatures. Prof. Blaze had shown them a dried-up shriveled skin once. That one was definitely spoilt. To find an unspoiled one he would have to be there when the tiger lizard was shedding its skin. As for the crystal eggs, shoggies lived by the seashore. Everyone knew that. There were thousands of them at the east end of the marsh – but how to tell one that was sitting on eggs, now that was another matter entirely. And shoggies were so big and heavy. How would he even get one to move to see if it was sitting on crystal eggs?

The Guidance

Soot opened the pouch. He carefully unwrapped the contents, placing each pebble on the floor in front of him. He smoothed out the fine leather wrappings. The following guidance was etched into the leather:

The first wrapper:

> Do not lose courage in considering your own imperfections. Act in accordance with your heart not your fears and the miracle fibre will hold you aloft.

The second wrapper:

> Nothing is so strong as gentleness, nothing so gentle as real strength. With this you will prevail.

The third wrapper:

Kindness is the code. Think not of yourself but of others. Observe this and you shall reach the journey's end.

What kind of guidance is this! thought Soot. *No map. No - go here and then go there. How was he expected to go on a quest that gave him no start and no finish?*

Soot looked at the three dull gray pebbles he had unwrapped. He knew that the secret to a dragon's strength lay in his quest pouch and were connected in some way to these pebbles. But what exactly that connection was, he did not know. He thought back to his chivalry classes. Prof. Blaze had talked about the virtues a dragon must develop to be of service to the kingdom. Truthfulness, loyalty, and cooperation were high on his list. One must cooperate to get a job done. Yes, he could see that. That is how the dragons of Frith had raised Spoargum's pole. Fifty of the strongest dragons had dragged it up from the beach, the way swept clear by hundreds of flapping wings. Special rope had been spun from the gossamer of the giant red spider. A hole had been clawed out in Frith Stadium and the sticky, strong rope wrapped around the great pole as the dragons, each with a thread in their snouts flew into the air in unison erecting the pole and securing it in position.

He looked at the pebbles again. He rolled each one around in turn, pinched them and scratched at them with his clawnails. Brought them to his nose to smell but found that they were odourless. He curled up in his lair and thought about all the unusual and exciting things that had happened over the past few days and finally drifted into sleep.

The next morning, Soot woke to the wonderful aroma of smokum porridge. His mother was slowly stirring the porridge as it

bubbled up the sides of the large cooking pot. As she added the smokum berries she sang an ancient dragon verse.

Smokum porridge hot to taste
Best for eating when in haste
Smokum porridge in stomach stays
A tasty meal for seven days

"Good morning, Soot. I hope you slept well. Are you ready to start your quest? Is it a difficult one?" she asked.

"Very difficult, indeed, Mother," he said. She smiled. Of course he couldn't tell her what his quest was. That was forbidden. He might find help along the way but not prior to setting out on his quest.

"Follow the guidance, my son, and all will be well."

"I guess so," he said but he was far from convinced. Still he felt better after a heaping plate of porridge.

"Not too much, Soot," his mother, warned. "Too much smokum porridge will make you sleepy." She then went outside to have a look at the weather. The skies were a clear purple but she could see some green clouds over Harroby Marsh.

My! thought Soot. *That Smokum porridge really is delicious. Perhaps I'll have just two more snoutfulls. After all it has to keep me going throughout my quest.*

"If you're planning on traveling by way of Harroby Marsh," his mother said as she came back inside, "You'd best be off. There's more fog rolling in from the sea. Better cross the marsh while it's still clear." Soot hung his quest pouch around his neck and took one last look at his mother, his cozy lair and the comforting pot of porridge before heading off down the road towards Harroby Marsh.

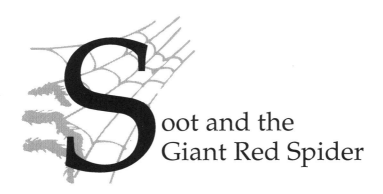

Soot and the Giant Red Spider

The morning breeze was picking up. Soon it would be strong enough to fly. *Things are looking up,* thought Soot. *I'll have a much better view of the marsh if I can fly over it.* He started to skip along the road and spread his wings out to be ready to take flight with the first strong up-draught. Taking off from land was still pretty tricky and he bounced along as he flapped, catching wind and then losing it again. Suddenly a strong gust came rushing under his outstretched wings and he was lifted high enough for his flapping to catch the air currents. He slowly rose higher until at last he felt safe enough to start to glide. He could see other dragons in the distance. He was not the only one heading for Harroby Marsh.

He flew over the area that had been used for the flame-throwing trials. He could see the scorch marks in the field below. A large colony of marsh beetles was busy gathering the bits of dried up grass, where the fireballs had landed. This type of crisp vegetation was exactly what they needed for their underground nests. Soot flew lower to get a closer look. The beetles were rolling the vegetation into balls and sticking the balls onto their prickly belly spikes. They waddled off to the opening of their burrow and made a clicking sound with their back legs. Immediately a female beetle popped up and took the balls down into the underground nest. The male beetle then headed back for more material. Soot continued on towards the edge of the marsh where the barbery trees and the moss fields grow.

Barbery trees grow tall and straight and are perfect for making dragon perches. He was starting to get tired and decided to land for a moment and take a little rest. He noticed some shiny silvery filaments hanging from the lower branches of one of the barbery trees. It was a tiny wisp of gossamer. *I must be getting close to where the giant red spiders are,* he thought. *I wonder how big they really are?* He spotted a nice rounded clump of moss and just couldn't resist doing a belly flop right into the middle of it. *I think I'll take just a little nap before proceeding further,* he said, as he closed his eyes sinking deep into the soft bed of moss.

When Soot awoke everything was a hazy gray. It was as if he was looking through a thin sheet of silk. He felt like he was floating above the earth on a cloud. He could no longer feel the bed of moss beneath him and when he tried stretching his wings they became tangled in the hazy film. As he gathered his wits and tried to figure out just what was going on, he saw a large, VERY large, red spider hanging from a length of gossamer suspended from the branch above him. He was not floating on a cloud. He was stuck in the web of a giant red spider! The web was stretched between two barbery trees. Every time Soot tried to move, the web bounced up and down but held him fast. Then Soot noticed another bundle wrapped in gossamer hanging from the branch. *I'm not the only one it's caught today,* thought Soot. There was a piece of yellow tail sticking out of the bundle, a dragon tail, and it looked very much like the end of Spark's tail.

The giant red spider lowered itself and started to examine its catch. It dangled close

to the bundle where Spark was entangled and grabbed it with two very nasty looking mouth hooks. Soot could hardly bare to watch. The spider turned the bundle round one way and then back around the other way. Suddenly the bundle started to squirm and quiver. There was a hissing sound and a puff of smoke. Spark was awake and very much alive. The spider reacted quickly by spinning the entangled Spark round and round, wrapping him in several more layers of gossamer. Very soon the struggle ended and the yellow tail hung loosely once again. *Poor Spark!* Then the spider swung over to where Soot was. Soot could feel its piercing orange eyes looking though the gossamer right at him. He kept his eyes shut tightly and lay as still as he possibly could. The spider grabbed him with its hooks and Soot thought he was done for. But he remained still and held his breath. Then it let him go and lowered itself to the ground and crawled away. *Yuck!* thought Soot. *That thing is horrible. I've got to get out of here before it comes back.* He started to wiggle gently to try and discover what parts of him had some movement. His wings were hemmed in by the sticky gossamer but fortunately they were in a slightly spread out position. This gave a little freedom to his front claws. His strong hind legs had been wrapped separately in gossamer and he couldn't move them hardly at all. He grabbed onto the sheet of gossamer that was draping his head and started to swing gently back and forth. Slowly he was able to build up a little swinging motion. Then he got an idea.

"Spark. Spark! Can you hear me?"

"Mmmh mmmh grrhm,"came the muffled reply.

"Can you see where I am?" Soot asked.

"Mmmh mmmh grrhm,"

"If you can hear me, wag your tail once. If you can hear me and see me, wag your tail twice." The yellow tail gave one long swing up and down and then stayed still again.

"I'm trapped in the web too. I'm going to swing by you. Try and grab me by your tail as I pass."

"Mmmh mmmh." The yellow tail wagged once again. Soot continued swinging back and forth. As he built up enough momentum to swing by Spark he shouted.

"Now! Now!" The yellow tail swung out and wrapped around a hank of the web that Soot was caught in and the sticky bundles attached to each other.

"Good – now maybe we can work together to get free." Soot started to pick at the fibre with his clawnails. He teased it apart and slowly made a small slit in the surface so that he could see better and was able to start to open up Spark's bundle. The clawnail that belonged to his father had become razor sharp and was able to cut through even the very thick layer of webbing surrounding Spark.

"Wow! How did you do that?" asked Spark as his face was cleared of the sticky webbing. Soot smiled and showed him his clawnail.

"My secret weapon," he said.

"What?"

"No time to explain. We've got to get out of here." As soon as Spark's claws were free he started to help in the unraveling. They had to be very careful because they were suspended from quite a height and needed to work together to open up enough of the web to break free but still have it support their weight. Spark undid Soot's hind feet and Soot undid Spark's hind feet. They heard a rustling among the trees.

"Quick! The spider is returning." They climbed back up the gossamer fibre and onto the branch of the barbery tree. Their wings were covered with the sticky web. They gently blew hot air on each other's wings to help dry up the gossamer. They could see the shadow of the giant spider approaching. Their wings were barely dry but they launched themselves into the air and flapped furiously to get themselves airborne. It took a lot of effort but it worked. They flew several dragon breaths away before coming to rest on the east shore of the island. Only after he had landed did Soot remember that he had failed to collect four lengths of gossamer. He looked at Spark and saw that he was still covered in bits of gossamer that had stuck to his scaly skin. He also had bits of the stuff hanging off his wing tips and stuck between his claws. Maybe he had enough after all.

"Do you need gossamer for your quest?" he asked Spark.

"No," answered Spark.

"I need four lengths." The two friends sat down on the beach together and gathered all the bits of gossamer into a loose ball. They then

slowly unwound it to form lengths of yarn. A
length of yarn was measured from the tip of
one's claw to the elbow joint. Fortunately,
Soot's front claws and legs were pretty short
and he found that he had just enough to form
four lengths. He hoped it would be enough to
satisfy Spoargum. He re-rolled the yarn and
tucked it into his quest pouch.

"I need to go back to Harroby Marsh and
collect four marsh beetles," said Spark.

"I know just where you can find them," said Soot. "Follow me." The wind off the seashore was quite strong and they both were able to take off without difficulty. Soot led the way and brought Spark to where he had seen the marsh beetles. Soot pointed down to a dark moving line, now barely visible because of the fading light.

"That's it," he said. "Down there." Spark headed down to the marsh floor as Soot wheeled around and started his long flight back to the east shore.

Shoggie Eggs

In the distance, Soot could see a thick bank of fog moving in from the sea. He flew faster. He did not want to be caught in a fog bank over Harroby Marsh. He could see in the distance the rounded backs of shoggies on the east shore gathered in tightly formed groups on the large flat rocks. The warm air rising from their bloated bodies broke up the fog wherever they were gathered. Great big holes formed in the fog over the shoggies. It looked as if the fog bank might disappear entirely but as it slowly moved inland it began to form again. The dark shadows of the evening soon blended with the green fog and swept over Soot. He became unsure of his direction and was starting to become very uneasy. But almost as soon as things became murky he felt a warm glow coming from his eyes. A soft red beam of light shone from his eyes allowing him to see his way forward. He could feel his father's clawnail tighten around the claw that it was attached to. The tips of his claw seem to be pointing him in a specific direction. Everything else was lost in the green haze. He was flying once again in a tunnel but this tunnel was red and he was alone. Fear gripped him. He felt that his body was too heavy, his wings were too small and that he was altogether not up for the task ahead. Then he remembered the guidance:

> Do not lose courage in considering your own imperfections.

Act in accordance with your heart not your fears..........

His heart was telling him that his father was indeed alive and not all that far away. If he could just keep going. He felt that his quest was connected to his father in some way. He started to feel hot air rising beneath his wings and he could hear the sea breaking against the shoreline. As he came closer to land where the shoggies were the fog cleared. Though it was dark he could see the outline of their great big bellies rising and falling as they slept on the rocks. He landed carefully about one dragon's breath from the colony. He swept out a nice comfy sleeping patch in the sand, lay on his back, curled his tail over his belly, folded his wings and fell into a deep sleep.

He was having a perfectly delightful dream in which he, Ember and Spark were barbecuing gizzard sausages around a fire with their quest pouches filled and ready to bring back to Spoargum. The sausages were fat thick and juicy and made loud hissing noises as they sizzled on the fire pit. One particular sausage was making a peculiar noise. It started first as a low hiss and then got more high-pitched with a pinging sound. The sausage was growing bigger and bigger and then POP! This woke him up with a start.

The purple moon hung at two dragon breaths over Skegg Island. It cast a pale light across the sea and onto the beach. All the shoggies looked like they were still asleep and then he heard the sound again. A low hiss that grew more high-pitched and then started to ping ping ping. It was coming from a shoggie lying at the very edge of the group. He moved a little closer to investigate. The shoggie was sitting on a large flat rock like all the rest of the shoggies huddled on the small islet of rocks at the tide's edge. But this shoggie had a large bulge on its broad bottom. Shoggies look much like a great big stretched out blob with a narrow dome and a fat bottom part. They have no eyes and one earpiece that can only be seen when they are actively listening. This shoggie had its earpiece stretched out listening to the hissing sound coming from its bulge. Soot could see that there was an opening in the bulge and something round and white was slowly coming out. The shoggie was laying

an egg! Then he could hear that ping ping sound again just as the egg popped out. As soon as the egg came out, the shoggie pushed it under its fat bottom using its earpiece like a sweeping brush. This was very exciting! Soot had never seen this process before. He was surprised at how small the egg was, not much bigger than a conker. No wonder it was made of hard crystal to protect it from getting broken while the shoggie was sitting on it. Several more eggs were laid in quick succession and then the shoggie pulled in its earpiece and sat quietly like all the other shoggies as if nothing had happened.

Soot moved a little closer. He was as quiet as he possibly could be. He had never been this close to a shoggie before. He wondered how he might be able to move the shoggie and collect two eggs without disturbing it. Dragon law protects shoggies. If he disturbed the group they would make such a hissing noise that the dragon guards who patrolled the beach would come and send him away.

Soot moved a little closer until his clawnails were touching the base of the rock. He arched his long neck over towards the sitting shoggie and tried nudging her over gently with his snout. She held firm as the rock she was sitting on. He tried a little harder and suddenly her earpiece shot out and almost hit him in the eye as it curved down towards his snout. He pulled back and sat ever so still until the earpiece finally sucked back into the shoggie's domed head. *How was he going to move her without disturbing the whole herd?* While he sat on the beach and pondered his predicament the tide started to come in and very soon his feet and bottom were covered with icy cold water. His wings started to shiver so he blew a little hot air over them to stop them from rattling and making noise. He felt a little better until he had an irresistible urge to sneeze. Rather than let his sneeze out he tried to swallow it. That almost worked but a stray jet of flame from the sneeze came shooting through one of his nostrils and bounced off the rock right beside

the shoggie. The shoggie slithered quickly to one side uncovering her pile of eggs. She hissed loudly as her earpiece came out and swept the rock looking for the eggs. Soot quickly picked up two eggs and put them into his quest pouch. The shoggie used her earpiece to sweep the rest of the eggs under her bottom. She seemed not to notice that two were missing and soon stopped hissing and settled back to sleep.

The Reunion

The tide was coming in. Soon the rock-ledge would be surrounded by water. Soot moved back onto the sandy beach. He was very tired. He had hardly slept all night. Still, he felt very lucky, more than lucky. He already had two of his three quest items and his quest pouch was filling up nicely. He decided to roll the shoggie eggs up in the spider gossamer. While he was busy packing the eggs, one of the pebbles fell out of the pouch. It was no longer a dull gray colour but now had a yellow tinge to it. He searched around for the other two pebbles and found that another one of them was now a bluish colour while the remaining one was still dull gray. Soot examined them closely and rolled them around in his claws. He could feel his father's nail tingle and glow warm when he touched the yellow and blue pebbles but felt nothing when he touched the gray pebble. The sun was just starting to crack through the dark horizon and its light shimmered across the sea. The ice was mostly melted but Soot could see that there were still several patches of ice floating in the middle distance between the East Shore and Skegg Island. One of the patches of ice looked darker than the rest and seemed to be moving towards Frith. Soot was drawn to the dark shape and sat on the beach staring at it. As it floated closer to shore, Soot could see that the dark ice was crowded with green shapes that looked like wingless dragons. *Glomgoyls!* thought, Soot. *I must find a conch shell and raise the alarm.* He rooted around the shoreline looking for the large conches that give off the loudest blasts. He found a suitable one under a large clump of seaweed. As he raised it to his lips he took one more glance out at the approaching ice-flow.

The creatures were now quite visible. There were perhaps a dozen in all, of varying sizes, mostly quite small and skinny looking. Not at all what Soot had imagined. At the front of this sorry looking crew was the largest of the glomgoyls. He stood leaning over the edge of the ice ready to jump as soon as the ice-flow hit dry land. His claws were curled around the edges of the ice-flow. As Soot placed the conch shell to his lips and took a deep breath, his attention was drawn to those claws with their long nails gripping the ice. One of the claws was missing a nail! The conch shell fell to the ground. Soot was shocked to his core. *Father – is it possible?* He lifted his claw and looked at the nail that had attached itself to him. It was throbbing and felt hot. He wanted to rip it off and throw it into the sea. He wanted nothing to do with it. But it was firmly attached and part of him. He stood transfixed to the shoreline unable to move as he watched the ice-flow bob up and down on each wave that brought it closer to shore.

Suddenly a large wave picked up the ice-flow and deposited it on the far side of the rock-ledge where the shoggies were sleeping. It smashed to pieces as it hit the rocks and the glomgoyls scrambled onto the ledge and crowded together in a frightened pack. They were all shivering except the largest one (the one missing the clawnail) who started to gently blow flame in an effort to keep the others warm. It was a small weak flame, blue in colour. Soot was completely bewildered. But but ... *glomgoyls can't blow flame.* He looked at the large glomgoyl again and saw that its skin was a very dark green, much darker than the others and that it had a pair of large but shriveled wings that hung loosely by its side. *Father? Is it Father?* .... Soot waded out into the water, jumped back onto the rock-ledge and started to waddle and weave his way between the shoggies to get close to the glomgoyls. He didn't care whether his father was a glomgoyl or not. He just wanted to get close to him. His heart was thumping loudly and his clawnail was throbbing and aglow.

"Father, father," he croaked, as he came closer.

A hundred shoggie earpieces shot out as they became aware of the intrusion. They started a hissing noise that grew louder and louder as their earpieces swiveled around and sensed that there were glomgoyls on the rock-ledge. In the distance Soot could hear a conch shell blowing. The alarm had been sounded. He started to run and skip along the rocks.

"Father!" he shouted above the din of the shoggies. The shoggies had started to stampede and clamber off the rocks into the water to get away from the danger they had sensed. Soot could feel the water level on the rocks climbing with each wave as the tide rose higher and higher. If he didn't take flight soon he would no longer be able to as the water would be too deep. The glomgoyls were all huddled on the one remaining large boulder.

Soot sprang into the air and flew the short distance to the boulder, landing right beside his…father! They recognized each other instantly. Soot put his snout under the left wing of his father, just as he had done many times as a very small dragon. The smell was full of the earthy smell of his lair with just a hint of the smell of his mother cooking smokum porridge.

"My son, how you have grown into a fine dragon warrior," he said with tears in his eyes. "I am happy to have seen you one last time. Now you must fly away and save yourself before the sea takes us all. These dragons cannot fly and my wings have grown weak from years of imprisonment."

"I can carry you, Father. It's not far to the beach."

"I cannot leave them to perish on the rock alone." Soot looked at the pale green creatures, all of them smaller than him. He wondered why everyone was so scared of them. One of them belched and the smelly green bubbles coming from his snout reminded Soot of how hated they were.

"But why not? They're glomgoyls. They imprisoned you for years. They stole your quest pouch and all your powers."

"Not all my powers, my son. Though imprisoned I kept many of my Bremmen powers because I remained faithful to the dragon code. I have willingly surrendered these powers to you that you may survive. Do you not realize that your recent strength has come from my clawnail? Now go! GO! A terrible storm is coming in from the sea."

The waves were climbing higher and surging up the rock-ledge. Small creatures were leaving their homes in the rock crevices and scurrying to the dry areas on the boulder. This rock-ledge had not been completely covered by the tide for eons. Crabs, beetle bops and lizards, hundreds of them were all swarming the boulder. Soot could see in the distance a legion of dragon warriors flying in formation towards the beach. He knew he had to get help. Just as he was springing into the air a small lizard jumped onto his hind claw and hitched a ride as Soot flew towards the dragon guards.

Friends to the Rescue

"Help! Help!" shouted Soot as he flew among the dragon guards. "My father is on that ledge."

"What are you talking about?" said the lead guard who happened to be Firecrest, Scorcher's father.

"That ledge is crawling with glomgoyls. We are going to make sure that none of them reach shore alive."

"But my father is on that ledge."

"If indeed your father is on that ledge which I doubt, he can fly ashore."

"But he has lost his power of flight," pleaded Soot.

"Then he has reverted to being a glomgoyl and will get no help from us."

Soot could see the cold steely glow in Firecrest's eye and knew at once that he would have to find another way to save his father. He flew back towards Harroby Marsh in search of Spark.

The sky over Harroby Marsh was full of young dragons in search of their quest items. He could see Scorcher and the Scarlew brothers heading towards the beach. *Oh no. Here comes trouble,* he thought as he flew back to the place where he had seen the marsh beetles. He was very relieved to find both Spark and Ember sitting on a mound of moss eating marsh beetles.

"I thought you were supposed to collect those – not eat them," he said as he landed on the soft moss beside Spark.

"Yes, but they taste pretty good. Don't worry, I have four already in my pouch – AND I have found my other two quest items so I'm done."

"Me too," said Ember. Both of them had their pouches hanging around their necks and they looked both full and heavy.

"I need your help right now," said Soot. "I found my father. He's stuck on a ledge with some glomgoyls and they will all drown if we don't help them."

"You found your father! That's great, but I don't think we can help glomgoyls. Can't your father fly to safety?" asked Spark.

"His wings have shriveled due to years of imprisonment. Please, you have to help me."

"Okay, agreed Spark and Ember. But how are we going to do it?"

"I'll tell you as we fly back. But hurry. Let's go."

The three friends stood on top of the mound and launched themselves into the air taking off with the ease of mature dragons.

"Spark, your fiery breath can protect our quest pouches. You can stay on the beach and guard them while Ember and I fly to the ledge." When they got to the beach Soot and Ember placed their pouches at Spark's feet.

"Okay," said Ember, "but I still don't understand how we're going to save them."

"We shall use the gossamer thread. It is as light as the air but strong as barbery root," said Soot. "It is the miracle fibre!" He passed Ember one end of the gossamer ball and they slowly spun it out into a long rope between them as they flew towards the ledge.

The waves were crashing against the ledge and a thick frothy green spray had covered its entire surface. The glomgoyls were huddled together with Soot's father standing between them and the waves. There was the sound of conch shells blowing from the west. The oncoming storm was blowing fiercely over Frith. The dragon guards had already left the beach to return to Spoargum's cave where they had been summoned for an emergency meeting. Soot and Ember flew low over the ledge allowing the gossamer rope to dip down where the glomgoyls could grab it.

"One at a time," insisted Soot's father as the terrified glomgoyls tried to all hang on to the rope at the same time. He gently restrained some while he encouraged the smallest one first to see how the rope would hold up. The little guy swung up on the rope like a monkey clutching it with his fore and back claws. Soot and Ember easily carried his weight between them and flew him to safety on the beach.

"Your flying has improved a lot," said Ember. "Is that really your father?"

"Yes," said Soot proudly. They returned and repeated the process until there were just two glomgoyls and Soot's father left. The ledge was now covered in water and up to Soot's father's hind leg joint. The two remaining glomgoyls had climbed onto his back.

"It's no use," said Soot straining with all the extra weight. "We can't lift you all at once."

"Please, Father, let them go and grab onto the rope before it is too late."

"If I put them down they will drown," said Soot's father. He lifted the remaining glomgoyls so that they could grab the rope just before a large wave swept over the ledge and knocked him into the foaming sea.

"Hurry, hurry," urged Soot. They flew back to shore and dropped the glomgoyls off with the others. Soot and Ember turned in unison and returned to where the ledge had once stood. It was no longer visible except for the swirling waves and foam that broke over the surface of the water covering it.

There was no trace of Soot's father.

"Father, father," cried Soot as he swooped down circling low over the area.

"Give me a sign that you're still alive, please!" Soot looked at his clawnail hoping that it would glow, get hot or tingle with some sign of connection to his father. But it looked and felt just like all the rest of his clawnails, cold and horny.

And then he saw a strange little creature scamper along his left wingtip. It looked like two lizards meshed together as one. Then he realized that it was a lizard in the process of shedding its skin – a TIGER lizard!! A bright orange lizard with dark stripes emerged leaving its old dark skin draped on the tip of Soot's wing. It leaped into the sea to start its new life as a sea creature. As it disappeared into the water a warm glow came from its body, lighting up the sea as it dove deeper. There at the bottom lay Soot's father. His wings flapped weakly beside him. *He's still alive,* thought Soot. *If I can just get a line around him.* He folded his wings and dove head first into the sea. He had never been in the water before, had no idea how to swim under water but somehow managed to plunge down to where his father lay. He quickly wrapped the silken gossamer thread around him and then tugged

on the line. As soon as Ember could feel the pull he started to tug against it, straining with all his might. Soot was now out of air and too weak to help. He floated to the top gasping and spluttering. He could keep afloat with his wings outspread but he couldn't take off. Watching from the beach, Spark knew his friends were in trouble.

"Don't touch those quest pouches," he warned the glomgoyls as he leapt into the air to help Ember. He took one part of the thread in his snout and pulled in unison with Ember.

They managed to get the thread to shore but it seemed only to have gotten longer and thinner and there was no sign of Soot's father.

"Keep pulling. Keep pulling," shouted Soot as he thrashed about in the water, half swimming, and half paddling with his wings as he made his way to shore. "We must be gentle. We must be gentle or the thread will break. It's being ruined by the salt water," he instructed as he got to the shore.

"But if we all pull together on a different piece of the thread we can do it."

As soon as the glomgoyls realized what was happening they each grabbed a piece of the line in their snouts and they all pulled together. And they pulled and they snorted and they pulled and they belched slimy green bubbles. And Ember and Spark and Soot pulled alongside them until slowly they managed to pull Soot's father to shore.

Now while all this was happening, Scorcher had arrived on the beach. He also needed shoggie eggs but by now the shoggies had all disappeared under water, which is what they do when sufficiently frightened. They were likely to stay under for days now that they had gotten such a scare. As soon as Scorcher discovered the three abandoned quest pouches, he quickly searched them to see what they had in them. He wasted no time in taking the shoggie eggs from Soot's pouch and transferring them to his own before flying away home.

The purple moon was eight dragon breaths over Skegg Island by the time Soot got back to his cave with his father. The time for completing the quest was over. All the cadets were expected to present their pouches to Spoargum on the day following the rising of the purple moon. Soot knew he had failed. Most of the gossamer had been left on the sea floor during the rescue of his father. Spider thread does not do well in salt water. He only had a few short threads left. The skin of the tiger lizard had been washed away when he plunged into the sea. His shoggies eggs had also disappeared. He had nothing to bring to Spoargum. Yet he was happy. He had his father home and that was all that really mattered. The wind howled all night long as the storm raged outside but Soot lay snug in his den surrounded by ten snoring glomgoyls. What a turn of events!

The Awards Ceremony

Next day the Frith arena was packed in anticipation of the return of the dragon cadets. The skies had cleared and the storm was over. The danger was past. The head dragon guard, Firecrest, announced that no glomgoyls had made it ashore.

"Furthermore," continued Firecrest, "our search party to Skegg Island confirmed that there is no trace of any remaining glomgoyls there. We conclude that all have drowned and that Frith and our treasured shoggies who keep the air free of fog are rid of the smelly creatures, once and for all time." There was a cheer from the crowd. Well, most dragons cheered. Some, like Prof. Blaze, remained silent. He never cheered at the misfortune of others and besides there was something peculiar in all of this, something that went against the code of truthfulness and fairness.

"Hmm – hmm, arrgh – arrgh," came the sound of Spoargum clearing his throat.

Firecrest bowed before him knowing full well that it was not his place to make such a pronouncement but Spoargum's, the supreme ruler of Frith.

"Very well, very well," said Spoargum, not wanting to be a drag on such a splendid day.

"Let the dragon cadets come forward with their quests."

One by one the young dragons came forward. Not all of them had managed to complete their quests but all of them were congratulated and encouraged by Spoargum for their efforts and bravery. Those who had completed their quests would join the dragon brigade immediately, while those with some items left would assist Prof. Blaze until next Phoenix when they would surely succeed with ease. When it was Scorchers turn, he swaggered forward with his head held high. He emptied his pouch out with a flourish and all his quest items tumbled out; one toadstool from Skegg Island (got fair and square), one live marsh hare, his hind legs tied so that he couldn't run away (captured for him by his father), and the two crystal shoggie eggs (stolen from Soot).

"Very impressive," said Spoargum. "I do believe that you may have won the prize for the most outstanding cadet of the eon."

"Excuse me, Lord Spoargum," interrupted

Prof. Blaze, "but there is one more cadet to present – Soot."

"What, what – where is he then," demanded Spoargum.

"Cadet number 13069, son of Stingfire and Fanfan, please present yourself," announced Prof. Blaze in a loud voice.

Soot who had been standing to one side, as he had nothing to offer Spoargum came forward and quietly laid his pouch at Spoargum's claws.

"Forgive me, Lord Spoargum, but I have nothing to offer you. My pouch is empty save for the three pebbles that were in it at the start of the quest."

"Hmm," said Spoargum. "The quest stones are yours for life. I ask only for the efforts of your quest. Did you not get any of the items I requested?"

"Well, yes I did, but – but I lost them."

"You got the gossamer from the giant red spider, then?"

"Yes," he answered.

"And where is it now?"

"It's at the bottom of the sea." The crowd laughed.

"A likely story," scoffed Firecrest.

"You got the skin of a tiger lizard, then?"

"Yes," answered Soot.

"And where is it now?"

"It's at the bottom of the sea." The crowd laughed again.

"I suppose those shoggie eggs you got are also at the bottom of the sea," said Spoargum who was getting quite annoyed.

"I don't know where they are," he answered truthfully.

"Why don't we ask cadet number 14089 if he knows where they are," suggested Prof. Blaze looking at Scorcher with a disapproving glare.

"Show me your quest stones now – both of you," demanded Spoargum.

The crowd gasped! A dragon was never asked to show his quest stones in public. In fact no dragon in Frith had ever seen another dragon's quest stones before.

Scorcher dropped his on the ground first.

"See, just as you gave them to me, my Lord," said Scorcher.

Then Soot tipped his out. Three glowing gems fell to the ground. The crowd grew silent. They had never seen such perfect gems.

"I'm sorry, my Lord," apologized Soot. "I don't know what happened to them."

"My dear young dragon warrior," said Spoargum. "You have done well – very well and I am pleased with you."

"I don't understand," said Soot.

"Your quest stones and their condition are a reflection of your heart. The quest is a test and a means to develop the virtues that will aid you in your service to the kingdom.

The quest items themselves are useless unless collected in the proper manner of the dragon code; with honesty, courage and kindness to all who may cross your path."

"Even glomgoyls?" asked a voice in the crowd.

"Who spoke out of turn?" bellowed Firecrest. "Come forward and beg Spoargum's forgiveness."

Soot's father stepped forward with ten frightened young glomgoyls at his heels.

They seemed a little less green now that they had spent some time above ground. Their skin was a bit tougher, less slimy and since they all had puffed and belched so much in their efforts to save Soot's father, their lungs were free of glomgoyl goo. One or two of them had small wing buds starting to sprout.

"What have we here?" asked Spoargum hardly believing what his eyes seemed to be telling him.

"Stingfire and the last of the glomgoyls," at your service said Soot's father as he bowed before Spoargum.

"Stingfire! Is that really you, my old friend?" asked Spoargum

"Yes, my Lord. It is I."

"Welcome. You are most welcome back to my service. But I'm afraid these glomgoyls can hardly be trusted."

"These glomgoyls showed kindness to me when I was imprisoned. These glomgoyls helped Soot, Ember and Spark pull me from the sea. These glomgoyls have done no harm to the kingdom and ask for your protection."

"Very well then. But you are responsible for them. They must swear allegiance to the kingdom and to the protection of all shoggies."

Spoargum waved his left wing to indicate that the interview was over and Soot's father returned to his place in the stadium.

"Now, could we please get back to the business at hand – the announcement of the Cadet Of The Eon Award? And the winner is.......

.... Soot, son of Stingfire and Fanfan; for his honesty, courage and kindness to all who crossed his path."

"Even glomgoyls," cheered the glomgoyls.

THE END

Nora Ryan's three previous works have been in adult fiction. Her Caribbean trilogy, inspired by her time living and traveling in the Caribbean is an exploration of social issues and spiritual themes. Dragon Quest takes her on a new journey as she travels into the mysterious and limitless world of fantasy. It is a world where young minds can expand and imagine a world full of possibilities, a world where they can reflect on their own challenges and the gifts that have been given them to meet these challenges and to pursue their own life quests.

www.noraryanbooks.com

Made in the USA
Charleston, SC
09 January 2013